WARNING!

Scaredy Squirrel insists that everyone brush their teeth with germ-fighting toothpaste before reading this book.

For my dentist, Rosa, and for Manuel

Special thanks to Valerie, my friend and publisher, for seven inspiring years

Text and illustrations © 2007 Mélanie Watt

This edition is only available for distribution through the school market by Scholastic Book Fairs and Scholastic Canada, Ltd

ISBN 978-1-55453-481-4

CM PA 09 0 9 8 7 6 5 4 3 2 1

Many of the designations used by manufacturers and sellers to distinguish their products are claimed as trademarks. Where those designations appear in this book and Kids Can Press Ltd. was aware of a trademark claim, the designations have been printed in initial capital letters (e.g., Godzilla).

Kids Can Press acknowledges the financial support of the Government of Ontario, through the Ontario Media Development Corporation's Ontario Book Initiative; the Ontario Arts Council; the Canada Council for the Arts; and the Government of Canada, through the BPIDP, for our publishing activity.

Published in Canada by	Published in the U.S. by
Kids Can Press Ltd.	Kids Can Press Ltd.
29 Birch Avenue	2250 Military Road
Toronto, ON M4V 1E2	Tonawanda, NY 14150

www.kidscanpress.com

The artwork in this book was rendered in charcoal pencil and acrylic.
The text is set in Potato Cut.

Edited by Tara Walker
Designed by Mélanie Watt and Karen Powers
Printed and bound in China

This book is smyth sewn casebound.

CM 07 0 9 8 7 6

LIBRARY AND ARCHIVES CANADA CATALOGUING IN PUBLICATION

Watt, Mélanie, 1975–
    Scaredy squirrel makes a friend / written and illustrated by Mélanie Watt.
ISBN 978-1-55453-181-3

1. Squirrels—Juvenile fiction. I. Title.
PS8645.A8845284 2007   jC813'.6   C2006-904829-0

Kids Can Press is a corus™ Entertainment company

Scaredy Squirrel

makes a friend

by Mélanie Watt

KIDS CAN PRESS

Scaredy Squirrel doesn't have a friend.
He'd rather be alone than risk encountering
someone dangerous. A squirrel could get bitten.

A few individuals Scaredy Squirrel is afraid to be bitten by:

walruses

bunnies

beavers

piranhas

Godzilla

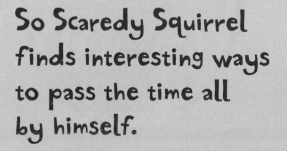

So Scaredy Squirrel
finds interesting ways
to pass the time all
by himself.

He reads.

He whistles.

He crafts.

He yawns.

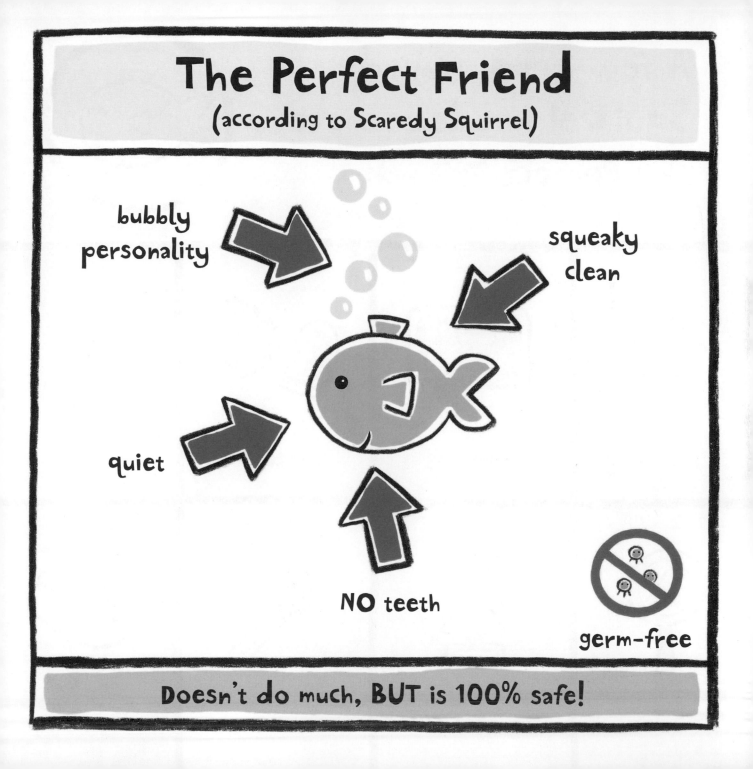

A few items Scaredy Squirrel needs to make the Perfect Friend:

lemon	name tag	mittens	comb
mirror	air freshener	toothbrush	chew toy

HELLO
my name is

Goldfish is here.

Avoid beavers: they could snap at any moment.

Watch out for Godzilla — for obvious reasons!

BUT let's say, just for example, that Scaredy Squirrel **DID** come face to face with a potential biter. He knows exactly what **NOT** to do . . .

DO NOT show fear.

DO NOT show your fingers.

DO NOT make eye contact.

DO NOT make any loud noises.

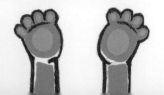

If all else fails, **PLAY DEAD** . . .

And hand over the Test.

Scaredy's Risk Test

1) Who are you?

☐ ☐ ☐ ☐ ☐ other ☐

2) How many teeth do you have?

2 ☐   100 ☐
10 ☐   1000 ☐
32 ☐   more ☐

3) What's your hobby?

biting ☐

other ☐

4) What do you see?

friend ☐   something to bite ☐

With every detail under control, Scaredy Squirrel puts the Plan into action.

First he tosses the chew toy.

Then he heads down the tree.

Everything is perfect until he hears a strange sound coming from behind:

SQUEEEEAK!

It's a dog!

This was NOT part of the Plan!

The dog chases Scaredy around the bush . . .

around the fountain . . .

Time out!

and around in circles . . .

until Scaredy Squirrel . . .

After all this time,
Scaredy Squirrel
realizes that the
dog doesn't want
to bite him ...

HELLO
my name is
Scaredy

He just wants a friend!

Scaredy Squirrel
points to his name tag
and smiles.

HELLO
my name is
Scaredy

Then he starts chasing his new buddy.

They play fetch.

They play hide-and-seek.

And they play dead.

Scaredy Squirrel forgets all about the goldfish, not to mention the walruses, bunnies, beavers, piranhas and Godzilla.

Time flies when you're having fun!

All this excitement inspires Scaredy Squirrel to make a few minor changes to his idea of a friend ...

pine
scent →

Buddy

Scaredy

P.S. As for the
wet doggy smell,
it's been taken care of.